Fancy NANCY

Poet Extraordinaire!

Before you know it, you'll be a poet!

Written by Jane O'Connor ✼ Illustrated by Robin Preiss Glasser

HARPER

An Imprint of HarperCollinsPublishers

In loving memory of my mother, who'd open *Magic Casements*
so many nights to share all her favorite poems with me—
including, of course, "Annabel Lee"
—J. O'C.

For my *Whale of a Tale* ami, Alex, with amore
—R.P.G.

"As Soon as Fred Gets Out of Bed" by Jack Prelutsky, text copyright © 1990 by Jack Prelutsky.
Used by permission of HarperCollins Publishers.
"Dig In" by George W. B. Shannon, text copyright © 2006 by George W.B. Shannon
used by permission of HarperCollins Publishers.
"First Snow" by Mary Louise Allen, text copyright © 1957, 1985 by Marie Allen Howarth.
Used by permission of HarperCollins Publishers.
"In the Motel" by X. J. Kennedy, copyright © 1979 by X. J. Kennedy. First appeared in *The Phantom Ice Cream Man:
More Nonsense Verse*, published by Atheneum. Reprinted by permission of Curtis Brown, Ltd.
"Picking Berries" by Douglas Florian, copyright © 2006 by Douglas Florian.
Used by permission of HarperCollins Publishers.
"Polliwog School" by Arnold Lobel, copyright © 2009 by the Estate of Arnold Lobel.
Used by permission of HarperCollins Publishers.

Fancy Nancy: Poet Extraordinaire!
Text copyright © 2010 by Jane O'Connor
Illustrations copyright © 2006, 2007, 2008, 2009, 2010 by Robin Preiss Glasser
Crayon drawings by Birgitta Sif Jónsdóttir and Anna Raff © 2010 by HarperCollins Publishers
All rights reserved. Printed in the United States of America.
No part of this book may be used or reproduced in any manner whatsoever without written permission except in the
case of brief quotations embodied in critical articles and reviews. For information address HarperCollins Children's
Books, a division of HarperCollins Publishers, 10 East 53rd Street, New York, NY 10022.
www.harpercollinschildrens.com

Library of Congress Cataloging-in-Publication Data
O'Connor, Jane.
Fancy Nancy : poet extraordinaire! / written by Jane O'Connor ; illustrated by Robin Preiss Glasser. — 1st ed.
p. cm.
Summary: Fancy Nancy and her class learn about poetry and write their own poems to read on Family Day at school.
ISBN 978-0-06-189643-9 (trade bdg.)
[1. Poetry—Fiction. 2. Schools—Fiction.] I. Preiss-Glasser, Robin, ill. II. Title.
PZ7.O222Fglk 2010   2009011606
[E]—dc22   CIP
                                                                              AC

Typography by Jeanne Hogle
10 11 12 13 14 LP/LPR 10 9 8 7 6 5 4 3 2 1
❖
First Edition

Bonjour, everybody!

I think poetry is sensational! (That's fancy for really, really terrific.) Even the word poetry sounds so beautiful and fancy to me.

Every day my teacher Ms. Glass reads our class a poem. My favorites are the funny ones. We are also writing our own poems. My best friend, Bree, wrote one about hiccups. You can read it. (Bree is very creative—which is fancy for full of imagination.)

Love,
Nancy Clancy

(My name rhymes, so I am naturally poetic.)

A POETRY SURVEY

Our class is doing a survey, which means you ask a bunch of people the same question—"What is your favorite poem?"—and then you write down their answers.

Here's my sister's favorite. I asked Ms. Glass if nursery rhymes counted as poems and she said, "Absolutely!"

MY SISTER'S POEM
DIDDLE, DIDDLE, DUMPLING

Diddle, diddle, dumpling,
My son John
Went to bed with
his stockings on.
One shoe off,
one shoe on,
Diddle, diddle, dumpling,
My son John.

I took this photo.
My sister is pretending
she is John.

My dad's favorite is "Blowin' in the Wind" by Bob Dylan. It's a song, and the lyrics—which are the words—also count as poetry.

Mrs. DeVine, my neighbor, grows all kinds of flowers. Her favorite poem is the very first one she learned when she was a little girl.

MY DAD'S POEM
BLOWIN' IN THE WIND

MY NEIGHBOR'S POEM
DIG IN BY GEORGE SHANNON

Dig a little.
Dig a lot.
Dig a brand-new
garden spot.

Plant a little.
Plant a lot.
Plant the seeds and
bulbs you bought.

Wait a little.
Wait a lot.
Wait much longer
than you thought.

Pick a little.
Pick a lot.
Share the best
bouquet you've got!

My mom loves poems that tell a story. She read "Annabel Lee" by Edgar Allan Poe to me. It's about a beautiful princess who has died and the guy who will go on loving her forever. This poem is so sad, it's tragic.

 Warning: I bet reading this poem will make you cry too.

I called my grandpa. He likes limericks. They are funny poems that always have five lines that rhyme.

This is the one I liked best.

MY GRANDPA'S POEM

A circus performer named Brian
Once smiled as he rode on a lion.
They came back from the ride,
But with Brian inside,
And a smile
    on the face of the lion.
    —Anonymous

Grandpa and me

(Anonymous means nobody knows who wrote this. There are lots of fancy words in poetry!)

Today we make a poet-tree in our classroom. (Get it? Poet-tree sounds like poetry.) Each paper leaf will have a poem that we composed—to compose something means you wrote it yourself. We're going to read our poems on Family Day.

I haven't written mine yet. I want it to be great.

Here's Bree's poem.

Horrible Hiccups
by Bree

Hic hic hiccups
Make my tummy jump in and out.
I hold my breath
Till I turn red. . . .
Hic— It didn't work.
I hate hiccups.

Here's what Ms. Glass wrote to Bree.

I hate hiccups too!
Your poem makes me think
you had hiccups while you were
writing it!

CLARA

C ookie crazy
L ovable
A rtistic
R unny nose
A merican

Ms. Glass showed everybody how to make a poem out of our names. You write the letters in a column and then for each letter you think of a word that describes something about you. Here's Clara's. (She was getting over a cold when she wrote it.)

PALACE OF POETRY

Maybe you already know that Bree and I have a club. We look for insects and other interesting stuff in nature. Now, after school, we go to our clubhouse to write poetry.

We call it our Palace of Poetry.

INSPIRATION

We don't talk much, but sometimes we put the radio on. Music often gives you inspiration. (That is a *très* fancy word for something that helps you get good ideas.)

HERE IS WHAT YOU NEED

A notebook (a glittery cover is good for inspiration)

Beautiful, soft music

A pen with a plume (that's fancy for feather)

Bouquet of flowers

Plenty of refreshments, because it's hard to be creative if you are hungry

Bree wrote this poem today. Now she can make another leaf for the poet-tree at school. How come writing poems is so easy for Bree?

Fighting with My Brother
by Bree

I wasn't ready
To read to Freddy
Or play a game,
So he called me a name.
I told my mother.
She got mad at my brother.
Now Freddy was sad,
And I felt bad.
We made up that night.
That was the end of the fight.

Later I tell my mom, "I am stuck!
I can't think of anything good to write.
Everything sounds stupid!"

My mom says, "Take a relaxing bath. Close your eyes and I bet
an idea will pop into your head."

So that's what I do. I add lots of bubble bath for inspiration.

I stay in the bathtub for a long, long time. When I get out, I am very clean and my fingers are all prune-y, but I still don't have a good idea for a poem.

WRITER'S BLOCK!

When I tell Ms. Glass about being stuck, she says, "Oh, that's called writer's block. It happens to everybody. It'll go away."

Here's what else we talk about.

A poem doesn't have to rhyme, right?

That's right. Bree's poem about hiccups doesn't rhyme.

So is anything a poem as long as the words are in short lines?

No. Poems are special. The words have rhythm and are fun to read aloud. Often a poem makes a picture in words.

Then Ms. Glass says, "You're a creative girl. I'm sure you will write a wonderful poem."

I am not so sure about that.

After school, I want to go straight to the Palace of Poetry.
But I can't. We need to find a birthday present and card for
my grandfather.

There are so many birthday cards, it is hard to choose.
Nearly every one has a poem inside.

There are also cards for special people—like a best friend
or someone who's sick. Suddenly I get an idea
for a poem—an idea that is superb.

GUESS WHO?
by Nancy M. Clancy

Her earrings dingle-dangle.
Her hair is never in a tangle.
Who can it be? It's Ms. Glass!

If I have any troubles,
They pop like bubbles
When I go talk to Ms. Glass.

I think I am a lucky girl.
I have the best teacher in the world.

You know who it is—it's Ms. Glass!

At home, I sit down with my notebook and my pen with a plume. Little by little, I get inspiration.

On Family Day, I read my poem. I read with a lot of emotion—that's fancy for feelings.

Later Ms. Glass whispers, "I am so flattered. What you wrote, Nancy, is called an ode. That's a poem that says what is special about someone."

An ode? How fancy!

Anytime I find a poem I love, I put it in this book I'm making.

Favorite Poems of Nancy M. Clancy

(I actually don't have a middle name, but I like to add M. because it looks fancy.)

In the Motel
by X. J. Kennedy

Bouncing! bouncing! on the beds

My brother Bob and I cracked heads—

People next door heard the crack,

Whammed on the wall, so we whammed right back.

Dad's razor caused an overload

And wow! did the TV set explode!

Someone's car backed fast and—tinkle!

In our windshield was a wrinkle.

Eight more days on the road? Hooray!

What a bang-up holiday!

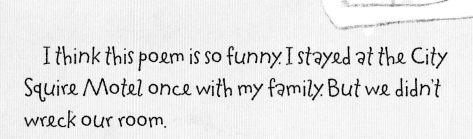

I think this poem is so funny. I stayed at the City
Squire Motel once with my family. But we didn't
wreck our room.

Five Little Pumpkins

by Anonymous

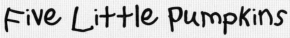

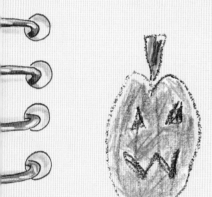

Five Little Pumpkins sitting on a gate,

The first one said,

"Oh my, it's getting late."

The second one said,

"But we don't care."

The third one said,

"I see witches in the air."

The fourth one said,

"Let's run, and run, and run."

The fifth one said,

"Get ready for some fun."

Then whoosh went the wind,

And out went the lights,

And five little pumpkins rolled out of sight!

Picking Berries
by Douglas Florian

Picking berries is very fun

Very berry merry fun.

Extra-ordinary fun.

Cherry cheery berry fun.

This is a tongue twister. Read it aloud.
You'll see what I mean!

First Snow
by Marie Louise Allen

Snow makes whiteness where it falls.

The bushes look like popcorn-balls.

And places where I always play,

Look like somewhere else today.

Polliwog School
by Arnold Lobel

Underneath

The lily pads,

Where the mud is cool,

Many little polliwogs

Swim their way to school.

"We go to class each day,"

Said one.

"And all we do is wiggle.

We do not read . . .

We do not write . . .

We only squirm and giggle."

Polliwogs
turn into frogs!

That rhymes!

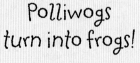

As Soon as Fred Gets Out of Bed
by Jack Prelutsky

As soon as Fred gets out of bed,

his underwear goes on his head.

His mother laughs, "Don't put it there,

a head's no place for underwear!"

But near his ears, above his brains,

is where Fred's underwear remains.

At night when Fred goes back to bed,

he deftly plucks it off his head.

His mother switches off the light

and softly croons, "Good night! Good night!"

And then, for reasons no one knows,

Fred's underwear goes on his toes.

Ms. Glass is right. Poems can be
about anything—even underwear.

I wish I had a poem about a tea party,
because I have tea parties all the time with
my doll Marabelle Lavinia Chandelier.
As soon as I find one I really like,
I'll add it to my collection.

Did you know that a collection of poems is called an anthology?
Isn't that about the fanciest word you've ever heard?

Start an anthology of your own. It's fun!